I want to hear music

that makes me feel something,

even if

what I felt was

pain.

Other books by
MICHAEL R. GOODWIN

SMOLDER

THE LIBERTY KEY

PRICE MANOR: THE HOUSE THAT REMAINS

STORY COLLECTIONS

ROADSIDE FORGOTTEN

HOW GOOD IT FEELS TO BURN

STORY SINGLES

THE RITUAL

BROKEN JUSTICE

KINDNESS

SPARROWS

CRIMSON GROVE

THERE ARE WORSE THINGS

A SHORT HORROR STORY BY
MICHAEL R. GOODWIN

Published by Dark Pine Publishing.

Copyright © 2023 by Michael R. Goodwin.

All rights reserved.

Cover design and typesetting by
Dark Pine Publishing.

www.darkpinepublishing.com

This is a work of fiction. Names, characters, businesses, places, events, locales, and incidents are either the products of the author's imagination or used in a fictitious manner. Any resemblance to actual persons, living or dead, or actual events is purely coincidental. This book or any portion thereof may not be reproduced or used in any manner whatsoever without express written permission except for the use of brief quotations in a book review.

For Jessica,

In my life, you are the b

THERE ARE WORSE THINGS

The record store was empty, except for me and the cashier, who was elbow deep in a bag of Funyuns and enjoying the Peter Frampton song playing far more than any sober human should.

"Isn't that wild, man?" he bellowed, a spray of saliva and crumbs coming from his cracked lips. He had to yell to be heard over the music, which was cranked to a volume not recommended for Frampton. "Hear that? It's called a talk box. It's this tube gadget that you attach to your guitar. Kind of like this!"

I had been trying to ignore him, but I instinctively looked up from the discount cassette tape bin I had been sorting through. He stuck the straw from his Big Gulp in the side of his mouth and grabbed the handle of a nearby broom, which he had abandoned when the current song came on. The cashier then proceeded to mimic the song, in turn making the experience of listening to Frampton more painful than normal.

I pulled the hood of my sweatshirt up over my head, but it did nothing to muffle the sound. If it wasn't for the bin of cassette tapes I was going through, I would have left as soon as the song came on. But this bin was like a haystack, and I was looking for its needle. I had this compulsion, and I was feeding it. Enduring the pain of this record store employee's horrific singing to get my fix, like any good junkie does. Except my addiction had nothing to do with drugs or illicit chemicals. My drug of choice was music.

I loved discovering new music. Listening to a new song for the first time was like losing your virginity. The opportunity to experience something new in a world that had begun to feel like a broken record was a unique type of gratification. I knew I wasn't the only one who liked to add new music into their auditory diet, but I didn't know anyone who did what I had fallen into the habit of doing.

Finding music that you've never heard before might seem like an easy thing to do. You walk into any record store and they're going to have a little of everything: pop, country, rock, jazz, classical, you know the drill. That wasn't what I was after. I didn't want studio albums produced by a team of audio engineers, because there are so many artists and singers that put out regurgitated versions of the same song. Throw in some new lyrics, change up the bridge, but at the core of it, they're all the same.

What I was after was the underground stuff. Obscure artists, garage bands, demo tapes… the more unheard of, the better. I want to hear music made by people learning how to make their soul sing. I want to hear the humanity that went into the music, not some garbage produced by the big corporate machine after they force their musicians to compromise their visions for the sake of profitability. I want to hear music that was made because it hurt the songwriter to keep the song within them.

Most music makes me feel nothing. Much of it is like eating without taste. It has no point, no destination. Music without meaning is like an oasis without water.

I want to hear music that makes me feel something, even if what I felt was pain.

So it was unmarked cassette tapes that I was after. Tapes that were made in such haste that they were not labeled or written on with a Sharpie. Tapes that were handed off and shared and ultimately forgotten, discarded. Tapes that wound up in the bottom of a box or a junk drawer and eventually migrated from one location to another like an old coin.

I had stumbled on the best way to do so: rummaging through the used cassette tape bin at record stores. Sometimes you came up empty, but usually there were one or two cassettes at the bottom that made my pulse quicken. It was a thrill, like what I'd imagine a man who bet on horses waiting for his horse to pull into the lead would feel, or a junkie waiting for the spoon to heat up.

That's how I came to be at Canal Street Music ten minutes before closing time, elbow-deep in a wire bin while Peter Frampton played overhead: on the prowl for my next fix.

It was 1983, and I was twenty-three years old. I had been hunting music for two years, and on this night, I found my prey at the very bottom of that wire bin: three unmarked tapes, completely void of any indicator of just what treasure (or trash) they might contain. They were old, dirty, and beat to hell.

Just the way I liked them.

The cashier, he of the Funyuns and the Big Gulp, gave me a look when I set the tapes down on the counter, as if *I* was the weird one.

"Do you even know what these are?" he asked. "They're not labeled."

"I know. Still want them," I said, rubbing my temples. I pointed back at the wire bin that I had gone spelunking in to retrieve them. "The sign says that they're three for a dollar. Doesn't say they have to be labeled."

The Frampton song blessedly ended and the cashier turned a dial underneath the counter to lower the volume. Apparently he wasn't much of a Led Zeppelin fan, but I tapped my fingers impatiently to the opening riff of *Black Dog* while I waited for him to comprehend my last statement.

"But there's no way of knowing what's on them," he persisted. "There could be anything on there. Like the Bee-Gee's or… Janet Jackson."

He said her name like it left a bad taste in his mouth.

THERE ARE WORSE THINGS

"Guess I'll find out when I get them home," I replied.

"Oh well," the cashier said with a shrug, and tapped a few buttons on the cash register. "It's your money."

"That, and the customer is always right. Right?" I faked a smile and handed over two crumpled dollar bills from my pocket.

"That's true," he said, "but in this case I can't say I agree."

He punched another button on the register and the drawer sprang out. He counted out my change, and dropped the coins into my waiting hand.

I shoved the tapes into my back pocket, gave him a close-lipped smile, and turned to leave. I was almost on the sidewalk when I heard the cashier say something to me. Halfway out the door, I leaned back in.

"What did you say?"

"I said I hope it's none of that satanic shit that they've been talking about on the news," the cashier said, genuine concern on his face. "You hear about that?"

I nodded. The nightly news and the newspapers had taken to calling an uprising of concerning events involving cults and ritualistic sacrifices the *satanic panic*. I didn't know much else about it.

"There are worse things," I said.

The cashier raised an eyebrow. "What could be worse than the devil?"

"Peter Frampton's Greatest Hits."

The cashier flipped me the bird with both hands as the door swung closed. I returned the gesture and headed toward my car.

* * *

I left Canal Street Music with two things: the beginnings of a headache and a trio of cassette tapes shoved into my pocket. My car was parked on the street, a risky thing to do in downtown Lewiston, and I half jogged over to it.

The parking spot I chose was under a lamppost, the arc sodium light buzzing as it spread out its jaundiced glow. The noise reminded me of an auxiliary cable yanked from an amplifier that had been cranked to eleven, the sound of raw energy waiting to become music. The light helped to deter any would-be thieves, not that anyone would want my shitbox Pontiac, or anything inside of it.

I fished my keys out and unlocked the door. As I was climbing in I saw the lights inside the record store shut off, and then the cashier exited, a large keyring in one hand and his Big Gulp in the other. He locked the door and walked away down the sidewalk. An idea occurred to me, so I reached for something under my seat.

I dragged out my cassette folio, flipped it open, and searched for the tape I had in mind. The tapes chittered in their brittle plastic slots, my fingers slipping over them until I found the one I was looking for, popped it into the deck, and fired up my car.

The cashier looked over his shoulder as my headlights came on, and then turned back when I started toward him. With one eye on the road and the other on the FWD button on the tape deck, I fast-forwarded the tape until I reached the track I wanted.

As I approached the cashier, I let my knees hold the wheel while I rolled my window down with my left hand and cranked the stereo with my right. The dulcet tones of Vince Neil blasted from my car's speakers, informing the whole block that he was shouting at the devil.

The cashier glared at me from the sidewalk as I slowed down to match his speed. He flipped me off again and said something that I couldn't hear. I didn't really care, as my mission was done. I had gotten my revenge for the migraine I was starting to call Peter, and now I could go home.

I switched off the Mötley Crüe and drove home in silence. My mind wandered, thinking about the tapes in my pocket, and hoping, for the love of all things good and holy, that they weren't bootlegged Frampton albums.

I'd had quite enough of that already.

Part of my routine when I went tape hunting was to always wait until I got home to listen to them. The speakers in my car were garbage, and I had ruined a couple of first-time listens that way. A song never hits as hard on the second listen. Even though you don't yet know all the nuances, you still know what's coming. For that reason, I vowed to listen to each tape at home, using the best equipment I could afford.

Listening to the tapes were first priority when I got home. Not that listening to them was pushing anything else that was important down on the list. I had few friends, no girlfriend, and I lived in a studio apartment that I kept fastidiously clean. On this night, as with many others that preceded it, I had nothing else better to do.

On entering my apartment, I headed straight to my desk. It was next to my bed, and I stored all of my beloved stereo equipment upon it. I kept my equipment covered by a blanket to keep the dust off. I pulled out the wooden chair and sat down. Listening to music, especially the new tapes I brought home, was always an exciting and reverent experience, something I approached with patience and respect. It was like taking communion, as it had become an almost ritualistic process.

A sheet of thick, gray felt covered the table top. My Onkyo tape deck sat in the center, a piece of high-end hardware that took me six months to save for. To its left was a small toolbox that housed specialty screwdrivers, in case I needed to disassemble or repair a tape prior to listening to it, as well as a variety of cleaning supplies. The Onkyo was flanked on the right side by a magnifying glass attached to an adjustable arm that culminated in a weighted base. Over it all was a lamp that housed several high-watt bulbs. I switched it on and then exhaled.

THERE ARE WORSE THINGS

Every tape went through an inspection process. Under the lens of the magnifying glass, I examined the first tape. With my eyes trained on the tape I reached out for the toolbox, flipped it open, and selected a screwdriver. The tiny screws in each corner were loose, and I carefully tightened them up. More of the same for the other two, so I snugged up those screws as well and then wiped them down with a cotton rag and gentle cleaner (a proprietary formula of my own making). The only thing left to do was to rewind them, which was done manually with the most specialized tool in my kit: the eraser end of a pencil.

I put my tools and supplies away and laid out the tapes on the gray felt, the anticipation palpable, building like static upon my skin as I placed my headphones over my ears.

The first tape contained narration which would, allegedly, help the listener quit smoking. The second was a recording of an old man reading the newspaper, his gravelly, monotone voice reminding me of my high school math teacher. He was reading the obituaries.

The third tape was, curiously, recorded backwards. A melodic baritone uttered syllables that sounded like words I knew but were spoken in a dialect that made them incomprehensible. I was about to shut off the tape when I realized that I was starting to understand it. Not the individual words, but more of the imagery that the sound of the words invoked.

THERE ARE WORSE THINGS

All at once the overhead lights flared up. It grew so bright I squeezed my eyes shut. I felt the heat from the bulbs on my skin and pushed my chair back just as the bulbs exploded. My chair tipped over and I tumbled off, shards of glass peppering my arms and the back of my neck.

My headphones ripped off, but I could still hear the voice, resonating inside my skull.

When I got to my feet, I was no longer in my apartment.

I couldn't tell where I was, but wherever I was, it was dark and it was *cold*.

The cold saturated me, numbing my fingers and toes. It was overwhelming and soon I was cold past the point of pain, cold past the point of awareness of much anything else. There was no sound other than my own breathing. The backwards voice was gone, and in the infinite cold and dark, I started to feel an overwhelming closeness.

And then... there was a new sound.

There was someone else in this space.

I heard the sound of bone creaking against bone. The survival instinct within me told me to run, but I couldn't move.

A hand with pointed fingers traced its way up my back, an unwanted caress. My limbs were frozen, leaden and unmoving from the immense cold. The hand grasped the nape of my neck, gently at first, and then with sudden and intense strength. My eyes, open and searching for whatever was in this liminal space with me, saw nothing. But as soon as my nerves were under pressure, my eyes exploded in brilliant light.

It was just white at first, virgin and pure, and then a snowy field came into focus. Twin ranks of towering high-voltage power lines cut black streaks in the sky, and there was an incredible noise, out of place for this desolate setting. Machinery, the chuffing of engines and clattering of metal against metal, made the ground and the air tremble.

The hand that had me by the neck suddenly pulled me down.

Down, down through the snow, through the frozen grass, through the dirt and clay and fieldstone. It was cold underneath the ground, colder than it had been in that field, and it was wet. The sounds of the machinery and their ceaseless digging followed.

The blinding white of the snowy landscape disappeared when we went underground, spots and streaks floated and faded in my eyes. I tried to blink them away as a miasma of sulfur and iron and decomposition made my nostrils flare.

We came to a sudden stop. Surrounded by the noise, the smell, and the cold, my ears picked up on the growing sound of drums. I envisioned little devils beating on drums made from human skin, using femurs as drumsticks.

I shivered, as the cold was in my blood now, rivers of glacial tides coursing through me with every slow beat of my heart. The hand on my neck finally released, but I couldn't move away as my limbs were still frozen.

The sound of the drums got louder, synchronizing with the machinery as both crescendoed to a point where I thought my eardrums would burst. And then, the cacophony started to diminish. It faded to near silence leaving only the drums, before a heavy crash rang out, the sound of massive metal doors being slammed closed and then locked.

I collapsed to the ground. I tried to take quick inventory of myself, but it was hard to judge my condition in this place. My arms were heavy and difficult to—

RISE, a voice in my head commanded.

The hand that had dragged me down here now picked me up. It shoved me forward and I noticed a low, burgeoning light.

I was in a vast subterranean cavern (*or crypt*, I thought), dimly lit by a fire that burned in the middle of the space. I turned to see who had brought me here, he with the sharp and pointed fingers, but I was alone. There was nothing in this space except for the fire, and a large, rectangular box.

A coffin.

THERE ARE WORSE THINGS

The lid opened and a skeleton climbed out. Its eye sockets were empty and deep, the guttering fire causing shadows to dance within them. What few teeth that remained in its jaws were sharpened to a point, the tips blackened with use. The skeleton walked toward the fire, which flared upon its approach and illuminated a large chair.

Not a chair… a throne.

The skeleton approached the throne, turned, and sat down. A rush of flames erupted from around the cavern as torches, mounted to the cavern walls in sconces made of bone, sprang to life.

The flood of light revealed an army of skeletons, human and animal alike, making their way in rank and file toward the growing fire in the middle of the cavern. Some carried drums slung around their torsos, using their hands to strike them. The cavern was soon filled with the thunderous sound of skeletal feet and hooves pounding the cold earth in perfect unison with the cadence being provided. Humans walked alongside stag and doe, bear and fox, and a variety of other beasts.

I started trembling with both fear and from the vibration of their marching. When at last the mass gathering of skeletons stopped, I heard screaming. It was a sound distinctly human, and I looked around to find its source. There, at the head of the aisle formed between the skeleton hoard and in front of the throne, was a man. My stomach plummeted when I realized that I recognized him.

It was the cashier from Canal Street Music.

Two giant skeletons held on to him with their massive hands. He struggled against his captors, screaming in fear and in pain, and for help.

"Please! Let me go! I'll do everything that you said, just please–"

A giant bone fist crashed down on top of the cashier's head and he collapsed to the ground.

THERE WILL BE NO MORE TALKING, a gravelly voice boomed, loud enough so it reverberated against the walls.

The skeleton guards stomped their feet to enforce the order, and I wondered why no one seemed to notice I was standing in the back of the room. Surely the skeleton sitting in the throne could see me, so why was I being ignored?

WE WILL SOON BEGIN, the voice called out.

I backpedaled slowly, distancing myself from the crowd. There must be a way out, a hallway or annex from where the army of skeletons came from. I ran my hand along the wall, hoping to find a corner or a seam that indicated there was a doorway. There was nothing, and I began to panic.

The cashier woke up and started screaming. I looked up and saw the throne was empty. The giant skeleton had a bony fistful of the cashier's hair and was holding him in the air by it. His feet dangled several inches above the ground.

THIS MAN WILL PARTICIPATE IN THE CEREMONY OF THE RIPPING.

At these words, the cashier stopped screaming. He was too terrified, too breathless to spend any oxygen on words. His lips moved with his continued muted protest.

The crowd of bones roared in excitement and… in hunger. Some jumped, their arms raised. Others stomped their feet, banged on their drums. The various animals among them pawed and scraped their hooves and paws on the ground. The sound was deafening.

THIS MAN GIVES US HIS FLESH.

The cashier thrashed, trying to free himself. He screamed and grunted, but still he dangled above the ground.

"No!" he screamed. "Please God, no!"

THERE IS NO GOD IN THE CELLAR.

The skeleton threw the cashier at the ground, and the sound of his ankles snapping echoed off the earthen walls. He clutched at his ruined legs, his long, pained moans filling the cavern.

THE MONARCH DEMANDS THE FLESH, SO WE MUST TAKE.

The cashier curled himself into a fetal position, wrapping his arms tightly around his legs. The skeleton guards grabbed him, each taking an arm. He fought against them, thrashing and kicking. His feet swung loose on shattered ankles, his screams of pain mixing with cries of anger and fear.

And then, from the far side of the Cellar, came another skeleton. It stood taller than any of the others, its bones a deep and weathered brown color. Scratches and gouges adorned its arms, and a deep groove wrapped around its left eye from the back of its head. The giant skeleton walked around the cashier until it was standing in front of him. They stood empty eye socket to wild, bloodshot eye. The cashier stopped his screaming, gasping for breath, still struggling vainly against his captors.

THE MONARCH HAS COME, the voice boomed.

In unison, the crowd of skeletons bowed deeply in respect. The sound of bone scraping against bone made me shiver, far worse than nails dragged across a chalkboard. Then, the cavern fell intensely quiet. The only sound was the crackling of the torches burning on the walls, and the great fire in the center of the space.

LET THE CEREMONY OF THE RIPPING COMMENCE.

The Monarch settled down into the throne. Even without the ability to convey any expression, I knew it was hungry. Ravenous.

The skeleton standing in front of the cashier lunged out and grabbed onto his

THERE ARE WORSE THINGS

face, its fingertips plunging into his cheeks. Trickles of blood seeped out as the sharp points of bone burrowed deeper. The cashier screamed, his pain renewed, and then the skeleton pulled down, ripping the man's face off his skull. It came down in two strips, splitting at the nose. Freshets of blood sprayed out as the skeleton kept ripping and pulling, revealing the glistening oily-red bone underneath.

The two skeletons holding the cashier by his shoulders turned and used their free hands to tear off the man's scalp. The wet sound of it separating from the man's skull turned my stomach, and I vomited at my feet.

The screaming and ripping continued as the skeletons proceeded to pull and tear off the cashier's skin and flesh from the head down. They pushed deep into his flesh with their boned fingers, stripping him clean.

On the throne, the Monarch watched. It was eager, impatient, a deep, ancient hunger radiating from it. The torches around the cavern flared up, yielding more light.

JOIN, the Monarch said.

All at once, the crowd of skeletons that had been standing at the ready rushed toward the man. They fought and struggled against one another, each wanting to get their share. They each wanted to rip off his flesh, to help turn him into one of them, another soldier for this skeletal army.

THERE ARE WORSE THINGS

Through the din came a sound, an undercurrent to the terrible scene playing out in front of me. It was that backwards sounding voice from the tape, the chant that somehow had brought me here. The images I had started to see in my mind while still in my apartment mirrored what I now saw before me.

As horrible as it was, I found I could not look away.

The many hands, skilled and eager to please their king, worked quickly. The smell of sulfur and iron made my nostrils flare, and the smell of spilled feces and stomach acid made my mouth seethe.

Despite the grotesque display and the horrid mixture of smells and sounds, it was the cashier's screaming that was the worst. It was unlike anything I had ever heard, a pure and animalistic sound that made all of the fine hairs on my body stand on end. It told the story of the unspeakable pain the cashier was enduring, and I wished for it to end. But when the cashier's screaming was finally cut short, the absence of it was somehow worse.

When it was all done, the legion of skeletons returned to their rank and file, covered in blood. The cashier himself, reduced to merely bone, now knelt in front of the throne. The Monarch's battered skull was angled downward, regarding the new member of its army.

THERE ARE WORSE THINGS

I realized I needed to find a way out of this place before they did the same to me, but before I could move, that bony hand clamped onto my neck again. I spun around and saw the Monarch, looming over me.

THE CEREMONY IS NOT YET COMPLETE, it said.

Without a second to react, I was grabbed by my armpits and dragged toward the fire raging in the middle of the cavern. I tried to free myself, thrashing my legs, succeeding only in knocking over a few of my captors until strong hands grabbed my ankles.

They threw me down in front of the throne as the Monarch was sitting back down. Terrified and breathing hard, I got to my feet and stood defiantly in front of the giant skeleton.

YOU ARE THE ONE WHO WAS SUMMONED, it said.

The tape, I understood, and its backwards chanting. Not quite *satanic panic* like the cashier had warned me of, but he hadn't been too far off.

YOU MUST NOW CHOOSE.

"What do you mean?" I asked.

The Monarch leaned down until we were face to face.

HE WHO IS SUMMONED MUST DELIVER SOULS TO THE CELLAR, OR SUFFER THEIR FATE.

No sooner had those words been said than I was yanked into the air. An instant later I was back in my apartment,

THERE ARE WORSE THINGS

dizzy and confused. My headphones hung from their cord, still plugged into my Onkyo with the tape still playing. I lunged forward and smashed the STOP button, the Monarch's final statement echoing in my mind.

Its missive was clear: doom myself, or deliver others to the Cellar.

My mind was a whirlwind, and I was exhausted. I laid down in bed, unable to sleep as the things I had witnessed replayed endlessly in my mind's eye. After what felt like hours, finally on the brink of unconsciousness, an idea occurred to me.

A horribly wicked idea.

* * *

Did you know that if you play *Stairway to Heaven* in reverse, Robert Plant sounds like he is talking about Satan? It's subtle and takes a little imagination, but it's there. Intentional or not, the phenomenon of backmasking (messages hidden in songs that you can only hear by playing the song backwards) was nothing new. Many bands purportedly had done it, and if bands with such esteem as The Beatles could get away with it, then so could I. After buying a few pieces of equipment, I got to work.

I don't know how many tapes I made, carefully blending the Monarch's summons into each one. Sometimes they were mix tapes, other times I re-recorded entire albums with that horrible backwards speech. I left them in public places, donated them to thrift shops, but I gave most of them away at work.

See, not long after my trip to the Cellar, I started a new job. One of my favorite haunts posted a job opening after one of their cashier's stopped showing up to work. I took over the night shift, and found that the patrons of Canal Street Music rarely turned down free tapes.

Music has changed a lot over the years, not just in sound but in its delivery. Cassette tapes were replaced by compact discs, and CDs by the MP3. Now, in the year 2023, streaming music reigns supreme. Vinyl has made a comeback, but regardless of the medium, the only way to stay relevant is to adapt.

I bought one of the first home CD burners so that I could continue my mission. When CD's started to decline and online file sharing became the rage, I made my MP3s available for download on Napster and Limewire.

As for me… I stopped looking for new music a long time ago. This task, this burden, ruined that.

I used to feel guilty handing out those tapes, but my mixes stream online now. I barely think about it. The only way I know any of it has worked is the fact that I haven't been brought back. As the idiom says, any day above ground is a good one.

THERE ARE WORSE THINGS

There's more truth in that than most people know, something I know firsthand:

There *are* worse things.

ABOUT THE AUTHOR

Michael R. Goodwin is the author of THE LIBERTY KEY, a novel of supernatural suspense, SMOLDER, a horror novella, and two short story collections, HOW GOOD IT FEELS TO BURN and ROADSIDE FORGOTTEN, and several short stories. His work has appeared in multiple anthologies.

Aside from writing, he enjoys spending time with his family, reading, composing music, and photography. He lives in Maine with his wife, their four children, and more animals than he can count.

Find out more information and purchase signed copies of his books on his website:

www.michaelrgoodwin.com

Follow him on Instagram:

@michaelrgoodwin

Printed in Great Britain
by Amazon